For Gonna

Copyright © 2012 by Jamie Harper

First edition 2012

Library of Congress Cataloging-in-Publication Data is available.

Library of Congress Catalog Card Number pending

ISBN 978-0-7636-4931-9

11 12 13 14 15 16 SCP 10 9 8 7 6 5 4 3 2 1

Printed in Humen, Dongguan, China

This book was typeset in Alghera.
The illustrations were done in watercolor and ink.

Candlewick Press
99 Dover Street
Somerville, Massachusetts 02144

visit us at www.candlewick.com

Miss Mingo
Weathers the Storm

Jamie Harper

CANDLEWICK PRESS

Early one April morning, Miss Mingo and her students gathered at the base of High Hill. They couldn't wait to hike to the top to visit the weather observatory. "I see you all brought your hiking gear," said Miss Mingo. "Sensational, class!"

As always, Alligator interrupted.
"MY mommy came to help!" she said.
"Do you like our matching outfits?"

"I'm here to help, too,"
said Cricket's dad.
"We're nuts for nature,
aren't we, Muffin?"

"I'd also like to welcome our new student, Groundhog,"
said Miss Mingo.

"Wow!" Frog said. "I heard that groundhogs are experts at predicting weather. So, Groundhog, what kind of weather will we have today?"

According to folklore, groundhogs can predict the length of winter weather. Their long hibernation has promoted the American tradition of Groundhog Day (celebrated on February second). If a groundhog sees its shadow that day, winter will continue for six more weeks. If not, spring is on the way.

"Today? Weather? Oh, perfect. It will be perfect."

The trail got steep in a hurry.
"Do we have to walk far?" asked Pig.
"When's lunch?" Hippo wanted to know.
"It's getting so hot," Alligator said,
huffing and puffing.

Frog studied the sky.
"Did you know that the sky isn't
blue on other planets? It's pink
on Mars, yellow on Venus, and
black on the moon."

When they stopped to rest, Cricket's father entertained the class with the sweet sound of his chirping. "The hotter it is, the faster he plays," said Cricket.

"Who knew?" said Frog.

A cricket's metabolism changes with temperature, leading to the differences in its chirp rate. As the temperature rises, the chirping speeds up. To estimate the temperature in degrees Fahrenheit, count the number of cricket chirps in 14 seconds, then add 40.

Meanwhile, Panda found a shady
spot to cool down.

In hot weather, pandas stretch their
bodies along branches and dangle
their legs over each side.

Hippo needed a rest, too. He was sweating buckets. "MISS MINGO," yelled Alligator. "Hippo's red all over— get some bandages. Quick!"

"Oh, dear," said Miss Mingo. "Don't worry," said Hippo. "It's not blood. It's actually good for my body."

When the weather is dry and hot, hippos secrete a reddish oily fluid called "blood sweat" from special glands in their skin. The fluid functions as a skin moisturizer, water repellent, and antibiotic.

Still, Pelican insisted on cooling him down.

"Are we there yet?" asked Pig.
"Smell those flowers,"
Miss Mingo said.
Snake slid through the blooms,
sniffing with his tongue.
He wondered why their
petals were closing.

Some flowers, like dandelions, clover, tulips,
morning glories, and chickweed, fold up their
petals before a rainfall. Their blooms tend to
be more fragrant just before rain.

Alligator was too busy tugging at
her clothes to notice the flowers.
"I'm so soooo sticky," she cried.
"Could be worse," Mrs. Alligator
whispered to her daughter.
"Take a look at Monkey."

"What?" said Monkey. "You've never had a bad hair day?"

Hair gets "frizzy" in humid weather because exposure to high humidity causes the hydrogen bonds in hair's protein to break, and the hair lengthens and expands. When the air becomes drier, the bonds form again and the hair shortens.

Frog noted the increase in humidity, too.
"Groundhog," he said, "do you think it's
going to rain?"
"It might. But it might not. Well, maybe
a little," answered Groundhog.
Frog studied the dark clouds hanging
overhead.

Clouds are not solid masses; they
are made up of millions of tiny
droplets of water.

"Hey, look," hollered Ant. "That's my auntie's house over there."
He called her name several times, but no one answered.
Her hill was very high and the door at the top was closed.
"Hmmm," Ant said. "I think it's going to rain."

Ants build and fortify their nests as rain approaches. They finish off by closing the entrance to the nest.

At that moment, something fell
from above.
"Hey! Who's throwing marbles?"
said Cockroach.
"They're not marbles," Ant said.
"They're hailstones."

The largest hailstone ever recorded
in the U.S. was a seven-inch-wide
chunk of ice — that's nearly the size
of a cantaloupe.

"TAKE COVER!"
cried Alligator.
Miss Mingo called
roll to make sure
the students were all
accounted for.

Flamingos have the ability to stand on one leg to conserve heat. The bird can lock its leg into a stable position and then stand facing any bad weather, such as rain and wind.

But some of the smallest
students didn't answer.
"Frog! Ant! Cricket!
Cockroach! Spider!"
she called. Then Miss
Mingo spotted them.

The phrase "It's raining cats and
dogs" isn't far from the truth. Strong
storm winds can suck up large
objects—record books tell of maggots,
worms, snails, frogs, and even snakes
being tossed around by the wind.

As always, Miss Mingo
knew just what to do.

As soon as the hail stopped, rain poured down. So the group
found a dry spot for lunch.
"Didn't someone say it was going to be 'perfect weather'?"
said Alligator. Groundhog kept eating.

Narwhal stopped eating his peanut-butter-and-sardine sandwich and lifted his tusk high up in the air.
"I think we should get going," he said. "I'm sensing cooler temperatures."

Scientists speculate that when a narwhal holds its tusk high up in the air, the long tooth serves as a sophisticated weather station, letting the animal sense changes in temperature and barometric pressure.

"Wait!" said Centipede. "I'll get a gazillion blisters if I keep hiking in these wet socks."

But changing into dry socks wasn't easy, even with a lot of help.

Narwhal was right. Chilly air crept in and covered
the hikers in an icy blanket.

"Groundhog!" yelled Alligator. "This is NOT perfect weather!"

Everyone was tired, but Bird inspired them to keep going.

"Louder, class," Miss Mingo cheered. "Sing louder!"

"Are we there yet?" asked Pig.

"It's getting foggy," said Narwhal.

"Well, actually," said Frog, "that's frozen fog."

The class couldn't see a thing. But Groundhog found
the nearest tree and crawled up to the highest branch.

"Rime ice" is frozen fog — it freezes
like snow, but it's ice.

"Miss Mingo," he called, "it's this way. Follow me, everyone. I see a rainbow — no, two rainbows!"

When a bright rainbow is visible, a second, larger rainbow can appear, parallel to the first. The colors in the outer one are fainter, and its colors are in the reverse order of the primary one.

Groundhog climbed down and led the way to the observatory.
Ranger Russ was surprised to see them.
"I'm so happy you made it," he said. "We're having crazy weather today."
"I'll say," answered Miss Mingo. Her students talked nonstop about all the different weather they faced during the hike.
"We learned a ton!" said Elephant.

"I suppose it's time to climb to the tippity top of the hill," said Ranger Russ.

The view was simply spectacular.
"There's my house!" shouted Giraffe.
"And our school," said Hippo.
"I see the dump!" said Cockroach.

Miss Mingo was smiling at her students when something landed on her beak.

"Is that a snowflake?" she said.

"Hey, Groundhog," said Alligator,
"You *can* predict the weather.
It's perfect!"

Pig was busy catching snowflakes when she noticed that the trail was disappearing.

"Do we have to hike ALL THE WAY BACK in the snow?" she cried.

"Follow me," Miss Mingo said. "I know a faster way."

AUTHOR'S NOTE

Little did I know when I hiked up Great Blue Hill with my daughter Grace's Brownie troop some years ago that it would provide the setting for a future picture book. On that day, much like Miss Mingo and her class, we climbed Blue Hill and visited the weather station at its peak. We met Don McCasland, who showed us historic weather instruments that are still in use today, and entertained us with true stories of extreme weather events that he had witnessed at Blue Hill. We learned that there really are places on Earth — some of them amazingly close to home — where you truly can encounter vastly different types of weather in one day.

The Blue Hills Meteorological Observatory was founded in 1885 by Abbott Lawrence Rotch as a private scientific center for the study and measurement of the atmosphere. Located just south of Boston, Massachusetts, the Blue Hills Reservation spans seven thousand acres; over one hundred hiking trails crisscross the twenty-two hills. Today it is a historic landmark where Don McCasland, the observatory's program director, continues to observe, record, and study weather.

Naturally, the research for this book brought me back to Blue Hills, where Don supplied a wealth of information. I'd especially like to thank Don for showing me the coolest weather instruments (my favorite is the hair hygrograph made with real hair to measure humidity) and aerial photographs of the Observatory. He took me to the top of the tower so I could get the very best view of the Boston skyline, and risked his life several times to take pictures from the rooftops that I needed for illustrations. But mostly I am grateful to Don for being so generous with his time over the course of the project. No one could have been more patient explaining the dynamics of a particular weather system, repeating it three, even four times until I finally understood. More information came from www.bluehill.org.

Many thanks to my daughter Lucy, who went hiking with me to Blue Hills one spring day to take pictures of the trails, terrain, trees, and wildflowers that I later used as reference for my illustrations. I was impressed by the thoroughness of her research . . . climbing into big, old hollowed-out trees, searching for insects under rocks, wading in a creek to find little critters, and climbing boulders and trees to get pictures from different perspectives. I will treasure that day forever.

Finally, many thanks as well to my daughter Georgia Rose, who came up with the idea for the cover of this book.

Photo courtesy of Blue Hills Observatory